# My Beautiful Voice

For the beautiful voice within us all – J.C.

In loving memory of Deborah Brash,
and thank you Davina – A.C.

Brimming with creative inspiration, how-to projects, and useful information to enrich your everyday life, Quarto Knows is a favourite destination for those pursuing their interests and passions. Visit our site and dig deeper with our books into your area of interest: Quarto Creates, Quarto Cooks, Quarto Homes, Quarto Lives, Quarto Drives, Quarto Explores, Quarto Gifts, or Quarto Kids.

Text © 2021 Joseph Coelho. Illustrations © 2021 Allison Colpoys.
First published in 2021 by First Editions, an initiative of Lincoln Children's Books, an imprint of The Quarto Group, The Old Brewery, 6 Blundell Street, London N7 9BH, United Kingdom.
T (0)20 7700 6700 F (0)20 7700 8066 www.QuartoKnows.com

The right of Allison Colpoys to be identified as the illustrator and Joseph Coelho to be identified as the author of this work has been asserted by them in accordance with the Copyright, Designs and Patents Act, 1988 (United Kingdom).

ISBN 978-0-7112-4830-4

Illustrated in acrylic paint and edited digitally

Designed by Zoë Tucker
Edited by Lucy Brownridge
Published by Katie Cotton
Production by Dawn Cameron

Manufactured in Guangzhou, China EB052021
9 8 7 6 5 4 3 2 1

Also available

# My Beautiful Voice

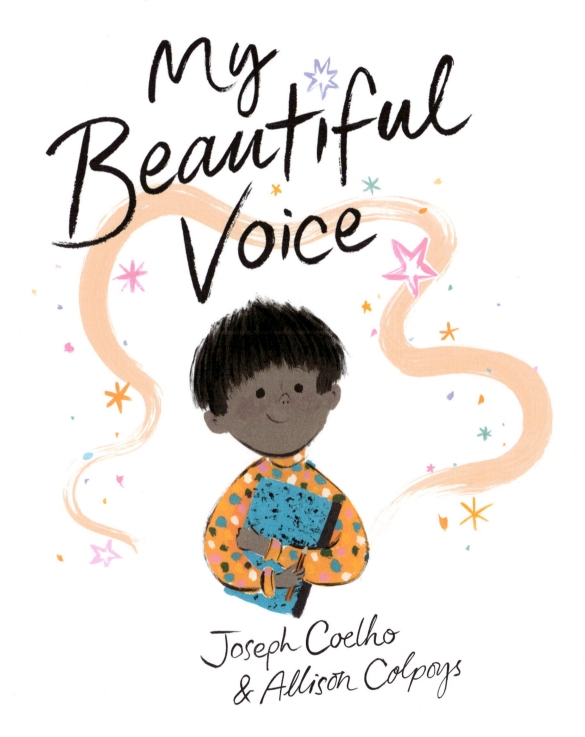

Joseph Coelho
& Allison Colpoys

Frances Lincoln
First Editions

The school is quiet.
New posters are
on the walls.

SCHOOL
POETRY
PERFORMANCE

READ YOUR
POEM
OUT LOUD!

My heart starts booming,
my skin becomes a raging river,
I feel scared and nervous inside.

But then...

Miss Flotsam explodes into the class.
She is our new teacher,
she has travelled the world.
Her clothes are...
   a flutter of fabric filled
with the spice of colour.
   And she loves poetry.

Miss Flotsam tells us stories
of cycle rides in
**booming** hurricanes,

boat journeys
down **raging** rivers,

flights through **scary** storms
and being alright.

When working in groups
on our poems
makes my heart flutter
and my face heat-up,

Miss Flotsam reads to me
stories of quiet heroes
and beautiful
unheard songs.

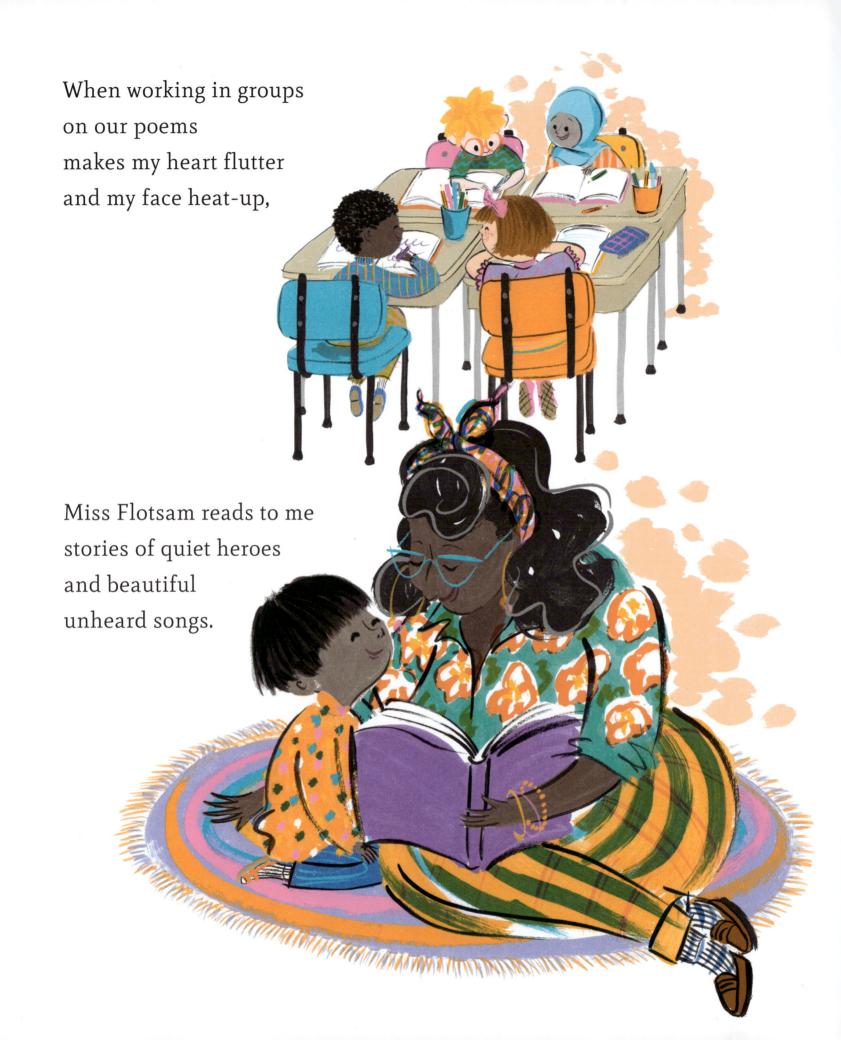

I write the first line of my poem.

When the other kids ask...
  "Why doesn't she speak?"

When fear and worry
freeze my mouth shut,
Miss Flotsam tells them...
"We all have songs to sing
and will sing them when we choose."

I add some rhyme to my poem.

When Caroline snatches my work
and teases me for never speaking,
her face like a blizzard,
Miss Flotsam gazes at her
with eyes that can turn thunder
into summer rain.

I add a verse to my poem.

Miss Flotsam performs to the class
all her travelling adventures:

like her search for
long-lost languages
in shut-up tombs

and finding new accents
in rainbow bustling markets

and discovering secret words
in dusty key-locked books.

I add the last line to my poem.

When my voice first arrives,
I'm not expecting it.
It comes out in a breath-of-a-whisper,
straight into Miss Flotsam's ear
and Miss Flotsam
just whispers back.
Like my whisper is a language
that only we speak
and she smiles when she speaks it,
and her hoops and bracelets
   tinkle and jangle
like a poem.

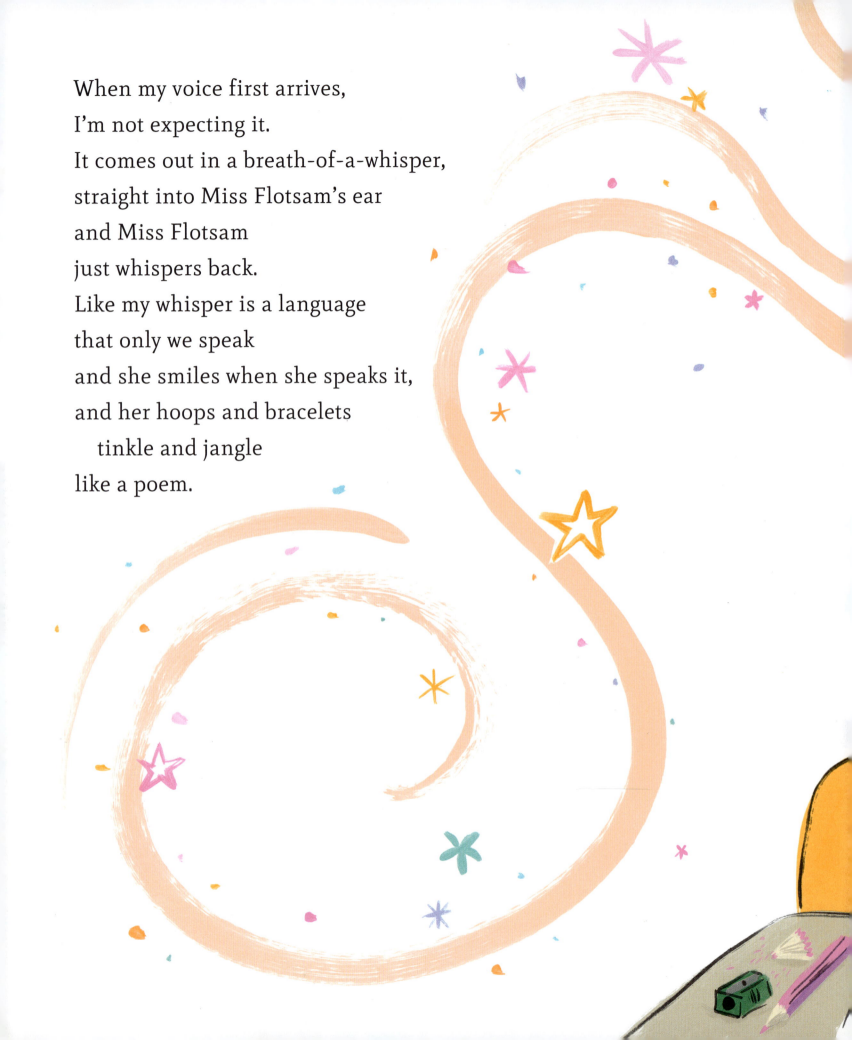

Our language of hushed tones,

of lines, rhymes and verses

starts bubbling up inside me.

My voice starts stretching its toes

and arcing its back.

When Miss Flotsam asks,
"Would you like to read
your poem to the class?"

I feel my voice inside me.
It feels like the first chirp of morning birdsong,
   like a key clicking in a lock,
like the first patter of summer rain,
   like the first call of a seller at market.
It feels like it wants to be heard.

I walk to the front of the class
and I feel like winds
  are pushing me back,
but I keep going.

I pass my classmates' desks
and I feel like I'm climbing a mountain,
    but I keep going.

I stand at the front of the class
and it feels like I'm at the edge
of a mighty cliff,

but I keep going.

My voice is rumbling in my belly,
vibrating in my chest,
and then the words of my poem
are streaming out of me,

riding my voice,
  filling the classroom,
tipping into ears,
  tinkling at the windows,
jangling on the desks.

The words of my voice
are whizzing around my smiling classmates,
zipping by a beaming Miss Flotsam
and I hear it for the first time,
and I realise that my voice,
    my voice

        my voice . . .

is beautiful.